Helma Oelwein

No Day is like any other!

A woman`s destiny at our time

Copyright:
© 2011 Helma Oelwein

Translator:
Reverent Bill Thalacker, Waterloo, Iowa USA

Editing:
Sylvia Angelika Oelwein

Design:
Grafikatelier by Andrea Mühl

Production and Publishing:
BoD - Books on Demand, Norderstedt

ISBN 978-3-752-66285-6

Dedicated to my great love:
my husband Kurt in memory,
to my daughters
Heidrun and Sabine in memory,
to my daughter Sylvia,
to my grand children
Isabel, Philipp and Julia,
to my great grand child Paul.

Foreword

I'm no Schiller or Goethe. I'm just a woman born in 1926. But my generation – not only me personally – has lived through a lot and experienced much. Through the chaos of war and with a sad and hurting heart I had to leave my Lower Silesian home. I am writing about my childhood – love – flight and expulsion, about life and death, which was often very close to me.

Faith – Love – Hope – who has not experienced that? It comes with the territory in all adversity.

If you are curious, read on.

Military training area in Neuhammer

I begin with my parents

My father Gustav was a cheerful, uncomplicated man born in a small village in Lower Silesia. After his schooldays he studied electronics. As a 21 year-old he had to go to World War I in 1914, from which in 1918, he returned home with gas poisoning My mother Marie was born in 1897 and learned dressmaking. Her parents and grandparents came from the so-called "Polish Corridor."

My parents were married in 1918. The first girl, my sister Elfriede, came into the world in 1920.

Thinking back, I recall how my Father came by his name Karl-Gustav Adolf.

His father Emil, was really happy to have a son, He had a very long way to go to get to the registry office, to enter his son into the birth register. For the trip he put a flask of the noble schnaps in his jacket and from time to time on the road took a little drink.

He was tipsy when he finally came to the birth register office. His son had still not been given a name. He tried to remember... what had he discussed with his wife? Then he remembered the solution: Wasn't the king of Sweden a large and more powerful man? Why shouldn't there also be something special from his offspring? So he was promptly named him Karl-Gustav-Adolf.

We later often delighted and amused ourselves with this re-collection!.

March 20, 1926
No Sunday Like Any Other

On this day the German government concluded a commercial treaty with Denmark and Portugal for both parties there were tariff concessions.

At Halle on the Saale the 3 national conferences of the Communist Party of Germany begin about the decisions about manufacturing. That opened a broad battlefront against the national socialist associations.

The first skyscrapers were to be built. But all that is not important today, and definitely not politics.

My mother was in labor and told her sister Emma: "Quickly make me a good sausage sandwich. Afterwards I get might not be up to getting anything to eat." It was shortly thereafter that as a healthy nine pounder, I saw the light of day. They wanted a boy as a second child, but nature had other plans. As it was told to me later, my father first wouldn't look, because it was again only a girl.

But I thrived splendidly in an intact family with a six year old sister.

My home was an average small town in Lower Silesia. Sagan was on the Bober River. It was a railway junction and home to the beautiful Wallerstein Castle. Sagan was located in the middle of the meadows and in vast forests and since 1844, had been the property of Duchess Dorothea of Tell.

The huge park was a gem with fountains, fountains and waterfalls, fountains spraying water, the cavalry stables, greenhouse, the Kings Bridge, and the artificial hills dazzled with the

Family picture with my grandmother who
came to see us often; also in the picture:
my father, my mother, my sister Elfriede and myself.

splendor of hundreds of roses and rhododendron species. The park was open and free for the public and every year was a feast for the eyes.

My parents realized very quickly that you can create more wealth by independence and were planning a move to a small place 18 kilometers distant that promised growth as a military training ground.

In 1928 in Neuhammer on the Queis they opened a textile and haberdashery. My mother had a sewing room. Also in the center of the store seamstresses gathered and tailored the articles that had been bought in the store. In this space there was the cutting table, where articles were measured, cut, and sewn. In one corner of the room stood a basket set, the table laden with pattern specifications.

Everything felt good in our new domicile. The landscape of Neuhammer lay in a beautiful setting and the river Queis, which rises in the Isar Mountains, had a funny current with lots of swirls. It had a very rocky bed, very clear water, but was to be treated with caution when bathing or swimming.

The Queis is the tributary of the Bober River, it rises in the foothills of the Jizera mountains, which come from the Sudeten. The water of the Queis is particularly cold, so the perch and pike have a good life there.

Back to business: There were also baby sets in the store with all accessories. I myself still "sucked" with greatest pleasure. I gave my mother no rest until I had pacifiers decorated with every possible color on a silk ribbon around her neck in which I could now alternately delight. That's how I had to occupy myself when the elders had been no time for me!

I often got a pair of scissors with rounded tips over my head and around my neck and you could often see me – as my grandmother later told me – with my tail stuck in the air in the big hat box. I had a firm footing and was determined to collect the different colored fabric scraps that fell off the cropping table.

Pacifier in mouth, scissors in small hand, what I must have unconsciously contributed to the amusement of everyone!

If I got bored with tailoring My grandmother often took us with her on a stroll to the small river meadows. One fine day before she could stop me, I couldn't resist the many pussy willows on the bank and slipped into the water. My grandmother got me out, sat me down and took off my pants and while I was crying, we finally hurried home. I was wrapped in the long skirts of my grandmother. That was my first introduction with something so cold and wet. It was probably the reason that later I wasn't very much interested in swimming!

The Queis River was an invitation to go boating.
Opposite you see the elementary school, where I was educated for for eight long years. The boat rental was busy in the summer. Our small town there didn't offer many distractions.

The red room in the Duke's castle in Sagan.
All the other rooms were wonderful! As I look back, many memories improve because how many times we admired the beautiful treasures the Castle offered.

1930 – my grandmother Berta,
She often entertained with little stories that brought laughter.
Unfortunately she wasn't always with us, but when she was
there the stories she told were touching for me.

We lived in the so-called "Lower Village" in which also could be found the public school with a large room, which belonged to the local hereditary noble. At the edge of the village there ware some farmers' farmsteads.

17 The year 1928 brought a very cold winter. The ladies had the special good sense and it was the fashion to be dressed in knee-length clothing with a belt draped around the hips. Women wore short hair, smoked in public and danced the Charleston.

Then great unemployment came over our country.

The Great Depression, the bank crash in America left its mark and changed a lot of things.

Even my parents had to now write their customers billing letters and staggered their purchases from week to week!

They also closed the business, so as not to be swept up in the general wave of bankruptcies. My mother was looking ahead for us girls and got full linen trousseaus ahead of time before being told to sell out.

I still remember getting white Damask bed linen which was embroidered with yellow butterflies and graced with a bouquet of purple violets. They were set apart for our dowry.

We then moved to be by others in the upper village. My father became an employee at the army garrison administration of military garrison at Neuhammer and my mother stayed at home to continue to serve their loyal customers.

Many years there were masked balls and I have wondered what became of the huge carton in which the remains of the store – masked costumes for rent – was stored. I strutted around the house in a clown suit. Unfortunately a neighbor gave me a tobacco pipe with tobacco and a light and I experienced too early in my own body, what tobacco smoke can do!!

I, Helma, strutted around the house in a clown suit –
Do you recognize me?

A picture of her parent's house.

Rose colored plastering – as my mother always emphasized, a brown painted fence, on the left was a group of outbuildings, about ten meters long. It housed a laundry room, two wooden stalls and two toilets, since running water was indeed a dream. In the house was a pump for the well dug at least 20 meters deep.

Meanwhile, my parents bought a plot of 2000 square meters at the edge of the village, located close to woods, and it soon began a brisk construction site.

In 1932 the completion of our own home was celebrated. There was a huge bowl – as big as a small bathtub – of potato salad with garlic sausage. A keg of beer was furnished for the industrious workers. I can remember the Polish workers telling funny stories and singing merry songs that fascinated me. Some were probably not be suitable for children's ears and when that happened my mother said somewhat firmly: "That's enough. Now people, go home, the party's over!"

It was naturally a small disappointment for me to have to go the long way to school that took probably about a half an hour to walk to the lower village

I was already big enough to go by myself, to Schauder the baker, or when I had a cold to the drug store or to Kalis the butcher. But it made me really mad when the butcher's wife said of my appearance, "Well, little one, you haven't washed your eyes well." That always upset me and my mother had to go to all the trouble to explain to me that what she meant my big dark big eyes had gotten her attention. When I looked at myself often in the mirror, I could find nothing special...

My father was often very funny, especially when he had been drinking a little. He then continued his circular saw on – the straw hat of the year – detected a frying pan or whatever he could grab and played an imaginary little song. My mother, however, didn't really appreciate that and said reproachfully: "Gustave, behave yourself!" Then he usually chose the song of "Little Mary sat crying in the garden..." which she naturally also did not like and she arched her eyebrows very high.

Then came my school introduction to Easter. Would my beautiful leisure come to a speedy end? No, for there was an involuntary prolongation – I got measles! I was speckled all over like a guinea fowl. As a consolation, I got a huge chocolate Easter bunny with colorful little eggs and a bag, which I remember fondly to this day.

I wasn't going to be getting out of going to school. But school only turned out to be half as bad as I had thought. I easily got everything set before us. I was very curious and sucked everything up like 22 a sponge. The Sytterlin script was like a beautiful painting, in which I indulged with devotion.
Calculating I found less interesting, but I slipped through all the elementary school year without trouble.

My first day of school. 1932

Picture of Helma on her first day of school with a box at her feet, holding a "Zuckertüte" holding confections / candy / school supplies / etc.)

My mother joined the "Women's League". There were days of sewing and the usual handicrafts We children played theater and here I am shown with

Hans Tronche of the Hagen, the son of the former camp commander. We gathered a lot of praise with our dance and I was summoned to the Villa, where this picture was taken.

I was very proud of my Biedermeier costume and wandered in with my suitcase for the reception. With blushing cheeks I then sat with my cavalier with cocoa and biscuits and felt great! A princesses could probably not have felt better.

We children playing theater.
Helma and Hans Tronche from the Hagen in theater clothes

The year 1933 came upon us with many political changes which in our little world were not immediately perceived or were evident. Adolph Hitler had a crowd of the faithful gathered around him – they wore brown shirts and armbands with the swastika. The old Hindenburg resigned and Adolf Hitler came as Reichs Chancellor at the top of the government. The youth were now to be more disciplined, the girls in 'JM' (Jungemadel / young women) up to 14 years and then in "BDM" (Bund Deutscher Madel / Association of German girls). We wore black skirts, white blouses and knotted ties.

The boys were "Pimpfe" [Ed. translator: This was a younger boys group.early and middle teens] and later were taken over in the "HJ" [Hitler Jugend – Hitler Youth. This was an older boys group..late teens and early 20's].

My friend from school Erich W., was a group leader who trained as a photographer and later recorded me, perched with pride in the bottom center of this image. It was he who offered to pick

This is a group picture which gives a glimpse into the serious discipline. Later "Military Training" was added.

me up from the weekly compulsory service in the BDM and safely to escort me home.

I didn't spend too much time with this meeting and still preferred the companionship of my big doll Elli, which in the meanwhile had the finest wardrobe,from bathrobe to dresses, costumes, clothing for balls, a wedding dress and even a fur-trimmed coat !

In looking back once again –
I should tell the story of the pig!

My mother was pleased that she could build a chicken coop at the front of our outbuilding, so that she could provide us with fresh eggs. In addition there were geese that had a fenced outlet.

One day she decided, to feed a pig to be slaughtered.

What was discussed was done! The pig was therefore purchased from the farmers, the butcher who came to the house, ordered the pig and made all the preparations. The great day for the slaughter drew nearer, in the laundry room the water was boiling in the boiler and we children waited, curious to see what would happen next.

The butcher now led out the poor pig, which got wild and broke away and darted at a gallop around our pump in the middle of the yard! Everyone was yelling on all sides! It took quite a while before they lay hands on the pig again.

Now my mother had taken on the task of beating the blood for the future blood sausage. However, for she was completely overwhelmed by the task. So she let the whisk stand and sought refuge in the laundry room. My father then took over the work after being so shamefully left in the lurch in the first place. Boiled pork, sausages and liverwurst, blood and bratwurst were the result of the slaughterhouse and the butcher took ham and other cuts 26 for smoking. The diet of the family was thus secured for the next few months, becausevegetables and potatoes from the garden were also plentiful.

After thinking it over, my mother announced, "Gustav, pigs will no longer be slaughtered in my house."

The great day of my confirmation came. In our church in Dohms I was confirmed with the memory verse: "Be faithful unto death and I will give you the crown of life."

Confirmation 1940
"Be faithful unto death and I will give you the crown of life."

My mother often gave us girls small jobs in helping with the work in the house. When my sister and I were doing dishes after lunch, I was supposed to be drying the dishes. There was a lot of nagging when just at that moment I had to "urgently go to the toilet". My sister, of course, wasn't pleased with that. However, when our various complaints got to my mother she usually ended it by saying: "Stop it," or "I'll just do it alone" The pedagogy was valuable because this was precisely not what was intended. That was my mother, she really didn't like strife and arguments.

My father had an air rifle and he thought a girl also would have to exercise good judgment and know how to use it. I was happy that we now had green cucumbers and tomatoes from the garden to serve that were stuck into the back garden fence and served as a targets. This was, however, an embarrassment to my mother, who did not approve of our doing that.

Meanwhile in politics all kinds of things were going on. The Nationalist Socialist Workers' Party had many supporters. Many of the unemployed were transients who came down the road. Marshes were drained. The government autobahns were probably the biggest project to be tackled. But things got better. There the "will work for food" time came to an end. Opponents of the regime were identified, we were told, "for re-education" in labor camps and Germany would be restored to its place in the world again after the war of 1914, after the defeat in 1918 and the troubling Treaty of Versailles. [Ed. translator: The promise was that Germany would be returned to greatness.]

Unfortunately, many pointed out that there would be a war, and in 1939 it happened. Much has been written about it and I do not want to repeat myself. I still remember to this day deep in the marrow of my bones Hitler announcing on the radio. "Since 5:45 we are now returning the fire."

The declaration of war was complete, the young men were called up for military service, the army was well equipped, but how was it going to end? How was little Germany to stand against such heavy odds?

In spite of everything living a normal life had to go on.

My parents agreed that the 2-year-old business school in Sagan would be right for me. Now I was taught typewriting (not the 5-finger search system) but exactly with 10 fingers as with the music clock. I really liked it.

We rode into town on a bus, which left early and brought the students back again at noon.

As to our family, I would have to say that my sister had married in 1938 and moved to Breslau where her husband worked as a police officer at an office.

In the summer of 1940, my father was conscripted to military service and he was assigned to the ground crew in an Air Force unit.

Food was rationed, so there were food ration cards. A efficient system had been built up unnoticed. But we really did not have any major concerns, even when my father wrote that he was now stationed in Sicily – the Italians were our allies!

1940

In the summer of 1940, anxiety and worry came like a car racing through the silent village. All households would have to evacuate immediately. Windows and doors should remain open and the residents should move immediately towards Sagan, since we were threatened with a large explosion.

We did as we were told, grabbed our bikes and headed out on the highway. After about one kilometer my mother remembered that she has forgotten her papers in an envelope that I was supposed to get quickly. So I raced back and in my great haste and hurry slid on my butt down our hallway...but I come back with the all-important papers, although I could hardly sit on the bicycle seat in pain.

We went to Eisen, and were housed locally and a few hours we could head home again. The danger was averted. The houses hadn't been destroyed, but the wind had blown all the curtains from the windows. It seemed quite adventurous for us.

The final story was that they had expected the explosion of the entire munitions depot. That was close!

My girlfriend Dora lived in the village opposite the post office over a watchmaker's shop known as Master William. We often met on Sundays.

At the open window sitting on a cushion – we looked out from the 1st floor to the bustle of the road. Sometimes a whole group of soldiers on break came over and waved to us and said things like, "Hello, you beautiful girls" or something similar. Even in these difficult times we already felt quite grown up, even older than other 15 year-olds.

One Sunday – it was no day like any other – a young Panzer man in his black uniform slowly walked over and looked up at us.

Dora said, "That man is shy."

When I went home that night – I went to assembly and was supposed to get home to my mother before dark to our house – I heard behind me measured steps. I hurried quickly to get past the woods that ran beside the road on the left.

It was the October 12, 1940 what a memorable day it should be for the rest of my life! My mother was waiting at the garden door and I hurried through it without comment. She looked around, however for who exactly were my pursuers...who asked harmlessly if this is the edge of the village.

They struck up a conversation. He introduced himself and said that his father lived in Potsdam and that he had come to train with the troops of his Panzer unit on a 3-week exercise.

My mother explained to him that there was no point in going an farther and on the spur of the moment invited him to dinner. There was of course potato salad with sausage!

What a surprise for me, that it was the shy Panzer soldier!

Now he began to appear on his off-duty hours, listened to my English vocabulary and so quite harmless tender bonds began to weave. We were even allowed to even go to the cinema, which was located in the camp and saw Hans Fallada in "Clothes Make the Man". I came home again safely, we we were tentatively holding hands on the last piece of the road! My heart was beating like crazy!

As we said goodbye, a faint "Goodbye" came over my timid lips and my heart fluttered like a butterfly. I could feel the blush in my cheeks and could not manage to hide this from my beloved. Smiling, he stroked my hair and gently kissed my forehead. I quickly disappeared behind the door of my parents' house without a backward glance.

When he moved away again with his unit, a lively correspondence started between us, because with the goodbye he had been personal and had given me the timid kiss that sealed our relationship.

His field post number was 28319 C – so many army postal parcels went on their way there.

How was a young girl, her head full of ideals and plans, to bring that about in such difficult times as the war years in 1941? Many things now went differently than a person could ever have dreamed. Despite everything, we are glad that in the business school the plan to study English remained, even if it was the language of our enemies. Maybe this was a small positive step in the big wide world? What was going on in our heads? The war affected everything, but we in the country didn't notice that so much as the city dwellers who were afflicted by enemy bombing. Life and death are both so close together! It's a terrible pointless thing that in a war so many people's lives are sacrificed.

After a good school year, I had to report to a "compulsory year" of service that no girl could avoid. So I came to a family with four children, the oldest was 13, the youngest 11/2 years old. The little one, "Puppi" was very ill. The little sweet brat was a lot of fun for me. After the wife, who hired me to do anything, realized I wasn't stupid I was in charge of almost everything in the house. I also sewed clothes for the children. I liked what I was doing, but in retrospect I must say that I was shamelessly exploited.

I was just 14 days from the my vacation when Gitte, the eldest, came running crying to my house. She said I had to come at once, that "Puppi" was very ill. The sweet little thing was pale

*12th of October
1940 – this is
how I met him*

and gasping in the crib. I ran quickly to the doctor who explained to me what she had and that he could do nothing more for her. I was in tears and cried all the way back to her. I sat down at her little bed and rubbed her cold legs as if I could thus give her new life. When the 36 doctor finally came, he said she'd suffered a stroke. There was a blue streak went from the back of the head down the neck. The housewife had a heart attack, the children all clung anxiously to me – but I was so helpless! I'd never been so close to death before.

The husband, who was somewhere in the military got 14 days special leave and took his wife for eight days to its location. I myself took care of the children and what's more, wasn't allowed to show my fear. I saw in each corner of my mind the little doll in her white frilly dress that I only recently had sewn for her and in which she was laid.

Then, after the families' difficulties with the budget and the responsibilities for a young girl like me, after discussing it with varying neighbors, my mother appeared. I finished my work there after six months. When the village group leader and my mother agreed to take into our home two vulnerable children from city bombing, I would get full credit for my missing half year.

That's how three siblings whom they did not want to separate, came from the Rhineland to our quiet house. They were six, ten and twelve years old. We had enough space. However, the little one was a bed wetter and so we had all kinds of experiences. My mother moaned often "Oh what I've given up." But this time passed and the children went back home. The time was without air raid alarms, without fear, and with good food. They had enjoyed the time with us because here in Lower Silesia we noticed and were affected only a little by the terrible war.

As you may see –
children become adults

Now things got serious! You had to have a job but there weren't many opportunities.

So I got a job at the Army building authority for Sagan and Neuhammer Branch, with job placement which was the registry in charge of where all the jobs were. There was a lot of variety in the work which I was happy about. So I was on the Army garrison administration staff, the Heeresstandortverwaltungsangestellte. Isn't one word a real tongue-twister?

In this department I was the only female among many men! My boss once said to me: "You are here to bring a more polite tone between all the employees. That's what a little lovely femininity can cause."

Before Christmas 1943 the Panzer radio operator came – now a Sergeant and officer candidate on leave after 19 months in heavy fighting in the vast expanses of Russia. Of course he stayed first with his father in Potsdam-Babelsberg. Then a few days were reserved for me. There was a wonderful reunion, because our mutual affection grew. We decided spontaneously, despite the uncertainty of the time of war, to have a life together. I was still terribly young, but our family has always been married very young. Even my grandmother had already gotten married at age 19. I consulted with "Papa Fiehn," an old medical officer, who saw an opportunity for him to go to into a local hospital because of his frostbitten legs and to go from there to the front line operation and that changed a lot.

A record made by my school friend-photographer who wanted me "in front of the camera lens"

1943
Here I am at the entrance to my Army administration office, Sagan Branch, Neuhammer Branch / Queis

Picture of Kurt Oelwein in his army uniform
As an unmarried man he would have to be with his troops
again on December 20 after having completed his holidays.
[Ed. translator: Because they were engaged they were allowed
to spend Christmas together]

1943 / 1944

So we could celebrate Christmas in 1943 a beautiful engage-ment, our engagement rings were secured by an exchange of old gold.

*The history of the engagement announcement
has had a long, arduous path!*

Despite all the hardships we spent a happy time, although every-thing in the background looked sad and disappointing.

After the daily treatments in the hospital he was often relea-sed. But to tell the truth, we didn't worry too much. That we took everything as it came is for me today almost more than I can understand. Now came a change for my fiancé with his dismissal from the hospital. He had to return to his service in a replacement company in Cottbus.

Also worth mentioning is that my tank radio operator had his back-up equipment in reserve at Cottbus and he was off-duty only on weekends. So he rode his bike which he had brought from Babelsberg, promptly every Saturday afternoon, the many kilometers towards Neuhammer. And you can't believe it! He rode on the highway!!

Around 4 o'clock I left from home on my bike and we met at a major highway exit. For him, it was a total distance of almost 90 km! Sunday night he went back home, because he had to wake up on time in the barracks on Monday. What an effort! But one of his return trips brought him some bad luck. The bike broke! Near the highway, he discovered a settlement, marched boldly into it and knocked on a door. You have to remember, it was three clock in the morning. An understanding older man felt sorry for the stricken soldier and lent him his own bike. He promised to repair the bike by the next weekend.

By the way, they exchanged to bikes without any problems.

As a result of the bombing raids on German cities there were countless names of the wounded and dead and smoking rubble. In our little village we could not quite imagine in what the form the terrible war would reach us.

We only had an air raid alarm one time because enemy aircraft strayed into our airspace. I remember that my mother and I were awakened by it and snipped beans in the garden by moonlight. That's as "seriously" as we took a air raid warning here!

After from 1939-1942 there was constantly only reported victorious advance of our troops. In 1943 the radio changed and corrected the image. Then there were set-backs and defeats! How could such a small country like Germany compete against the rest of the world? Was our government in the hand of a megalomaniac? The forces against us were superior to us in men and materials! How terrible that so many people have been needlessly sacrificed.

My fiance' was still in his reserve company in Cottbus and so we had the great good fortune to see each other on his off-duty weekends. But how could we be together like this? How long could we be together this time? It wasn't long before he had to return to his unit at the front. But well into June we were able to be together.

Was there something that might lighten the daily grind even a little? We were young, we had romantic ideas, and I had a marvelous idea!

We had in the office a microphone, with which we could communicate with the other agencies at the push of a button. Why not use it during work breaks for other purposes? I had so many beautiful songs in the back of my mind. So I sang to my heart's content, for example:

"It's all over, it's all over after each December following a May, goes back over everything, it's all over, but two who love each other, who remain true to themselves"

Or:

"Darling, my heart let you blow a kiss Only you with alone, I can be happy."

Or:

"A few tears I shall weep for you But you will not see it. But with goodbye I smile, because you can not see my heart."

Or,

"I am in love from head to toe, because that's my world, and nothing else".

There were very many songs, and my voice was greeted with enthusiasm and applause by all my colleagues. So I brought some color to our poorest everyday that otherwise was filled only with work and serious issues.

In all this, however, my thoughts were always with my loved one, doing military service in his armored division of greater Germany.

A transfer to Berlin, which seemed very tempting to me, was offered by our Heads of Service for three employees in a so-called draw. We had to take a shorthand and then type it correctly on paper. The stress was on accuracy and speed. What a celebration! I won the competition!! My mother was not very enthusiastic over my success, for now she stayed alone in my parents' house.

For me a new phase began. The Army Building Authority was dissolved and I was treated as a staff assistant to the Army High Command, briefly "OKH", assigned to Berlin. Since this service had already been bombed on Teltow-Ufer, we were working now in the Sperenberg mountain at Hegesee. We had lodging in a basement, always with two girls in a room. I was with a Anneliese Staubesand. We got along very well. We ate with officers and sometimes we fried something together on an alcohol stove. A small package often came from my mother which we very much welcomed. Once a package of smoked bacon came, which unfortunately had been a long time on the road. Lots of funny maggots crawled out... our visions of fried potatoes with bacon quickly became a dream!

There was much excitement there on the 20th of June: there was a coup against Hitler! But this was put down and many

Helma with an inflatable boat

Helma in her swimming suit
Life is beautiful in the harbor, life is beautiful at the sea.

participants were sentenced to death by the People's Court. If it had succeeded, would that have meant the end of the war? As things worked out, we had very strict rules and had to put in a lot of overtime.

With the nightly air raids, everyone going to the air raid shelter belonged to daily life. However, I often illegally stayed in bed. When a firebomb came down, thank God, a dud, I moved down the corridor, with my overnight bag to a bunker!

At the sea there was a so-called research company stationed that had to do with the development of inflatable boats. This often left us with yellow inflatable boats, with which we could sail on the water. We girls enjoyed the break, such as the two pictures show!

On the subject of war should also be mentioned that the German troops marched unopposed into Denmark. Norway on the other hand proved to be a bit more difficult, since the Luftwaffe played a major role. People spoke of a so-called blitzkrieg. In the West, Belgium and Luxembourg were surprised. Now even France was being overrun. On May 6, the armored divisions were advancing on and on, leaving the Maginot line behind them. In a few days the German army advance had reached the coast. Paris capitulated and the armistice between Germany and France was completed.

The advance in the East also went ahead and soon the German troops were standing in front of Moscow! But they had not had to deal with the Russian Winter! The advance came to a standstill. For months Stalingrad was shelled and the Battle of Kursk sealed the doom. The losses were monstrous.

Also in Berlin there was slaughter before and after the entry of America into the war from the RAF huge carpet bombing

I didn't know that I was already in the first stages of my pregnancy

over the city. Losses and destructions were enormous. On March 16 there were large-scale attacks by the Russians and the allies and no barricades could be made to hold them back. The end of the war became apparent.

When after the war, the Russian army occupied Berlin, a number of houses and villas were requisitioned by the military men. A Russian colonel led his crew into the house of my father-in-law. He himself was allowed to reside in two rooms upstairs and was allowed to use the downstairs kitchen. For this generosity he had only to thank his musical interest. Since he was an excellent pianist, he played the music composed by Russians before each day, pieces by Tchaikovsky, Beethoven and Rachmaninoff. So everything went in the best of terms.

The Russians got the food delivered to the house and he from time he had a drink of vodka with them.

A small disagreement happened there in spite of everything. One day the Russians complained of a stomachache and the housekeeper of my father was accused of mixing something into their food. God be praised there was an explanation for the malaise for the lords of the house, otherwise this may have been some very bad consequences!

Peace was restored again.

One day the house was released as this Russian delegation was moved to another location.

My future father-in-law had wondered if I could come on weekends to Babelsberg, but that was from Sperenberg and was often interrupted by air raid alarms. A half day trip was barely worth it. Once I sat for hours on that route somewhere in the bunker, the bomb explosion in my ears, and then returned went without completing the trip back to my site.

In the month of August 1944 I was overcome by the realization that I was pregnant, something of which I had not been aware up to that point, since I always had my irregularities with my period. How could I have been so optimistic [Ed. translator:

"blue-eyed")? I did not become aware of this condition, and yes, the pill did not exist at that time! I got the medical officer to approve five days special leave and went home, to a woman gynecologist in Sagan to clarify the matter. The finding was positive-and- this is a surprise! And not just for me! In the words of my mother, "This is a bit too early," My answer to their objection was: "Yes Mama, we can't help it. We've been engaged for so long."

Now quickly the war-time ceremony had to be organized for which we actually still had wanted to wait. Fieldpost letters went back and forth, special leave was arranged, and we met at the Silesian Station in Berlin, everyone drove with light luggage to my parents' house on the morning of September 28 where our wedding was prepared.

My sister, who had almost lost all their furniture in a bomb attack on Breslau had fled with her two young children back to our parents' house and now my mother had gotten started everything necessary for our hurried up wedding. Even my wedding dress was stitched and fitted wonderfully. My mother had somehow organized a shimmering dress: silk and lace that had been brought by my father from France.

I felt wonderful! Wonderful!

Our train station which was about 2.5 km from the town center, it was already dark, and what surprise – a closed carriage with two brown horses for our use. They had been found my mother on a farm in the neighborhood. From the open inside a gentleman tipped his hat and greeted us with a familiar voice. Incredible! It was my father! He had been at his unit in Sicily and gotten a special leave for his daughter's wedding. Inspecting my chosen for the first time he would say later that he had agreed with my choice already after his first conversation with him.

One day later, at Polterabend, in the evening we met my father-in law from Berlin, who had to climb over all every kinds of broken dishes in front of the house and in completely consternation said, "How does it look here?" [Ed. Translator: Polterabend refers to the marriage custom that the day before couples get married they throw dishes for good luck.]

Now it is up to the bride and groom, together to get rid of this "debris" or "Glücksbringer" [Ed. translator: "bringer of good luck"]. After the weary turmoil of the previous evening, we wanted to clean things up in the morning. But, lo and behold, my mother had already done everything. Hopefully this did our future happiness no harm? But we were both actually not superstitious!

30 September 1944 – was a beautiful autumn day like no other. We made our way to our Church in Dohm, who was 4 km away We had everyone put in three open carriages. We had no large wedding party.

The same pastor Brauer, who had confirmed me, got us married with the same text:

"Be faithful unto death, and I will give thee a crown of life."

My mother outdid herself with a exceptional wedding menu, although we still lived in a time of great scarcity! Our cook, Mrs. Krause, prepared a soup with egg custard and roasted goose with red cabbage, and dumplings naturally could not be missing. The crown of the menu was the dessert: lemon dessert with whipped cream! My father had brought with him from Sicily a whole box of lemons of which we barely knew. It was a

30 September 1944
A day like no other.

beautiful celebration with twelve persons that culminated with a dinner speech by my father.

A whole eight days preserved both our wedding holiday [Ed. translator: honeymoon], then we went back to separate responsibilities. There were the strict rules, you could not step out of line.

At the end of November my husband was wounded and came to the castle hospital at Hubertus Castle in Wermsdorf, Saxony. I was out of my office because of my pregnancy, and secured separate quarters there early in a rented furnished room to be near him. He had suffered a severe thoracic cage bruise and always got a giant bandage at the beginning of the afternoon. My room was so pathetically cold he stole three briquettes in the coal cellar of the hospital every day, so I wouldn't freeze to death.

We had however, in the village a favorite pub without rationed food stamps where there were potatoes with red cabbage or red cabbage with potatoes! A small coffee shop in neighborhood brought to us artificial coffee without brands, and carrot cake that tasted like straw. Despite everything, we filled ourselves very satisfactorily and we could still be together. Two days before Christmas, he was released and we went in an unheated vehicle on our journey home. We were now spoiled by my mother because I still had a terrible intermittent cough, which lasted almost to the birth of our first child.

My husband's sick leave came to an end, the war fronts looked bleak and hope dwindled for an end of the war. My husband went back to his unit and I was left to do everything possible to prepare for my baby. I bought a bassinet through friends, I lined it with delicate green lining. A good stroller from the children of my sister came as a gift.

We write now mid-January 1945

Suddenly now on our streets there are endless refugees were passing by using horse and buggy or often with just small hand-carts. They were between military columns on the way back from the front despite snow, slush and cold. Special trains had been put together for the people who were fleeing. Our tenant assisted those with little luggage. Her husband had to serve in the Volkssturm, the reservists.

Across from of us was a field hospital, in our house a colonel was quartered with his adjutant, we thus were in a war zone. Judging from the radio reports, although the Russians had broken through, they were still not close to us. However, this was not true! Operatively the enemy was already nearer than we believed. We now eagerly stored valuables and similar things like musical instruments, carpets, crystal, silver, porcelain – in the basement where we thought they would be safe. From the garden we picked up all sorts of boards and branches and in this way covered our wealth. My mother was of the opinion that looters would not find those things. Perhaps we could would get our things back when we returned home after fleeing the war!

My husband got in touch with me (what a miracle), by using a radio telephone. He was with his driver on the road, getting radio devices for his department.

He was hoping to eventually come close this way and take us himself. But this was a only a very wishful thinking; it wasn't in any way practical for that to happen, because the military police – called watchdogs – would summarily shoot every soldier who was without proper papers at the front!

49

Letters from my husband who was, of course, very worried
about us are at the back of this book.
These are letters from my husband, which grieved us.

I was now advanced in pregnancy, my sister had her two young children, there was my mother... what should we do? The last special trains had already left our station!

We now relied on our neighbor, although he suffered greatly from his asthma, but his truck was made ready with a trailer lining and he promised to take us.

So each of us packed a bedroll, a suitcase and a backpack. If there was a spare foot available we couldn't take any more to wear! I stuffed the stroller with baby clothes and emergency equipment that I had received from the NSA for a sudden birth, I was only 14 days short of the due date!

February 12, 1945 No day like any other!

On the night of twelfth we saw with horror, fires from a basement window and heard loud gunfire. The morning dawned pale and gray, we barely had a wink of sleep. Snow and slush were on the streets, our truck was ready for departure. But we still had to load two hundredweight sacks of potatoes and some canisters gasoline that our driver had long been hoarding.

Unfortunately, a canister ran out on the road and straight into our precious potatoes! What a misfortune! Now we all took our seats and went again into the village to pick up two women and the armed grocer as front passengers. As we now for the last time drove past our parents' house, my sister cried, "Stop, stop," Our driver braked sharply and we watched with horror just as a few quilts for the soldiers, our beloved gramophone and a stack of records were taken out of the house! My sister screamed: "Have you no shame? You're stealing from us when we have hardly turned our back" The soldier answered calmly: "Cool it, young woman, in the next few hours the Russians are going to be taking everything else out." It was only at that moment we saw the hopelessness of it all and the previously unshed tears began to flow...

I believe only at that moment it was clearly forced on us that we would be homeless. So far we had gone on without a murmur or complaint....just had done everything that needed to be done. I had tried not to get too excited by it all, but I always thought of my unborn child. Our Silesian song is appropriate here:

"On you Silesians, let's walk"

But what we could we expect in a foreign country? The future ahead was completely uncertain...

In a big bag I have old photos, jewelry, 3000 Reichsmark cash, a small pistol with six shells and some knitting placed on top of ammunition as camouflage, which should underline the harmlessness of the contents.

Some of the main roads have been closed due to shelling. We had to make detours, but we wanted to head west! It is a preview of things to come! Some streets are clogged with fleeing people and others with tanks, more tanks and soldiers.

After a few obstacles at 7 o'clock p.m. by the clock we reached Rothenburg and found a place to stay in mass quarters in a school. We all slept in the bare hallway. What a misery!

At 9 o'clock in the morning we prepared to proceed after we received from the Red Cross a cup of artificial grain coffee.

At 2 o'clock we are in Hoyerswerda and stayed in an inn together in a small space. We are seven adults and two small children. In the evening we got a couple of potatoes and cooked them a on a spirit stove. The cooked potatoes were a real treat for our hungry stomachs! The next day we heard of heavy fighting in our home area and the bad news reached us that all refugee flights are to be stopped and refugees are to be housed in tenements. We left quickly and went farther until after Königsbrück where we could spend the night in a school on straw beds. Our night was interrupted 3 times by air raid alarms. People suffered from diarrhea, and some could no longer get to the toilet in time. One can imagine the result – everything gets contaminated and it stinks!

Meanwhile, it was here that people injured by phosphorus burns arrived from Dresden. According to them, the city was only a smoldering heap of ruins! A terrible bombing by British formations had taken place. You heard only the worst news and now it's raining, it's raining, raining, raining...

Our co-driver with some luck organized a can of gasoline, because slowly our stock is running low.

For me, everything is currently very difficult, and yet none of these involuntary wanderings were at an end. When will my child come? Will it wait a little longer?

We still have a difficult trek. It is very mountainous and sometimes we get off to make it a little easier for the truck to climb the mountain. We arrived in Radeberg at midday but left it quickly because an air raid alarm was given.

In Zeithain our driver will go no farther because he's sick and his health is not good. Because of his asthma attacks he often has to endure an injection. We end up back in a mass quarters at a school, which is the plight of the homeless!

Out of pity I was allowed to sleep on the second night at the home of a young woman who worked there in the school kitchen. I was able to take my little nephew as there was a child's bed available. My fellow travelers could only sleep sitting up; everything was completely crowded that night.

But there are coincidences! Our co-driver, Mr. Berthold, found here in the hospital his wounded son and he persuaded us to stay here a few days.

We are plagued by doubts – was this break in the trip useful? Shall we give up our journey into the unknown? But where are we going? We had a hard time deciding.

Are we humans really just "dust grains on the edge of the universe," as it was once suspected a famous natural scientist? Every flower wilts, even the smartest person subject to this process. What will become of us?

Many questions went through our minds, for which I had no answers!

Lieutenant Scheuern who was known to me from the construction management site in Neuhammer went to a lot of effort to find private accommodations for us. He found an unheated attic room open for me and my mother.Despite cold, we were exhausted and slept well. What hardships the poor little thing must now go through in the womb!

After a general meeting with everyone, we decide to continue our journey because the local inhabitants will also have to move away.

On 26.2. our trip went through Oschatz, Mücheln toward Leisnig. The usual quarters for the night was on straw in a school – Then we would all meet again at the truck, unload some belongings, and then suddenly we travel farther: "In an hour we continue. Take the room key back again, otherwise all the refugees are to be in a special train to Bavaria "Goodness. Bavaria! Where is it? Shall we stay in some dormitories? No, that won't do for us."

So we go jump back into the truck and the bone breaking ride inside.

We drive on towards Leipzig and stop in Eilenburg. Once we spent two hours in a cold cellar for air-raid alarm – a very involuntary stay.

So we arrived in the evening in the town of Grimma. On one street a young woman appeared who was from our hometown. She found us a place to stay with her relatives. She takes us to one of her three aunts, where we could sleep in a nice soft bed! What generosity!? What a paradise! Should we now continue the gypsy life the next day Was this to be the end of the road? Silently everyone thinks we should stay.

Eventually our family separated itself from the traveling community. The good angel who took us in, who gave a room with two beds for the traveling community, was tireless. Mrs Ebert got us a cot, a bath, and other important items and made connections with the local midwife. Another aunt, 3 km away in Neunitz, which is located above the well, took my sister with her two little boys in their home because the woman herself was called up and the apartment was empty on weekdays. However, we needed to be identified as their relatives, because in our bureaucracy everything is complicated. Anyway in our misery we have gotten a stroke of luck!

It is now March 2, 1945

This was followed by registration with the authorities and receiving the food ration cards, back pay from our men in the amount of 163 Reichsmarks given and picked up as an advance. In addition, we got a loading authorization slip for three hundredweight of coal and many other suitable necessities.

How fortunate that at home I had withdrawn the 3,000 in currency from my savings book , which should make good services available for us in the future.

My health condition is relatively good and so the big coming event offered no gloomy shadows or anxiety. On March 3, I lost a lot of amniotic fluid and the next day I had a little labor. In the afternoon, the midwife comes and wants to help out with two syringes of something. At 6 p.m. I have very strong contractions, but the midwife is unreachable until she finally appears by 8 p.m.

Now the birth happened in quick succession: get out of bed, some squats are demanded of me. Too bad...all I wanted was to set a world record for lying down! Finally at 10 p.m. a little girl already lets out its first cry!

What a day – not a day like any other!

Did the little thing want to be born in that way in such a bad time?

The sweet thing is healthy enough to eat, is seven pounds, 51 cm long, has dark hair, which is combed right away. Yes, vanity among women is alive and well at an early stage. She smacks strongly on a little finger. That makes sense! Didn't she get nothing for months?

But how do you feel as a young mother, I was still so young that I couldn't believe the little miracle.

The next night there were two hours of air raid alarms, flak like crazy, that shivered the whole house and with it my bed. As we heard later, in a school there as the result of a direct hit there were 70 dead and injured.

According leaflets, a hard occupation of Grimma was about to take place. Hopefully it will not come true!

I had with great precaution made a bags with strong handles and wooden sticks at the top, in which I could put my child. It was sewn along the top in which I had a pillow, towel, diapers, undershirts, navel napkins, etc. for an emergency. In this way she could be transported effortlessly and stay warm in the basement in case of alarm. Really! But this happened only once!

Meanwhile, my baby, is now christened Heidrun Thea Helma. She is a particularly dear, quiet child. She drinks and sleeps and sleeps and drinks. I was doing well, except for the weight in the belly. I have the strange feeling that I've lost something, but something special has come from it!

On March 10, the little mouse is first bathed in the tub. The navel is healed and she liked the warm water exceptionally well.

On March 15, we have recorded a small bright spot: a postcard came from the field from my husband and my father also had a sign of life! How happy we were to know that they were healthy having come so far through this chaos of war. We only wondered how it happened, that the field post should find our current location?

We now had air raid alarms several times a day – we write the 6th year of the war.

On March 20, I had my birthday, as 19 year old, a young mother who did not really have enough time to be really grown up. So much responsibility at such a young age!

But as the saying goes: "We'll work it out somehow,"

Everywhere in nature, things were green and blooming and my heart was full of joy and confidence, Two letters came to me from my loved ones by way of relatives from Thuringia.

From the 5th to the 7th of April in Grimma literally all hell broke loose! Several bombs and direct bombings did significant damage. Were they probably intended for the nearby big city of Leipzig?

The Americans are now 40 km from our city – the city council called on the residents to store food for that time. People stood up to six hours deep in lines in front of the shops, bakers baked all night, and there was an excited chaos. The end of this insatiable war seems within reach. But maybe peace would be just as horrible?

Today, on April 14, I was in the city to get some necessities. On every street corner is a soldier or a Hitler-youth or a Peoples' Reservist with a bazooka ready to fight to the last man!

Meanwhile the American armored troops surrounded the city from every direction. And though the city defense commander, the city was surrendered.

My little pocket-sized yellow diary that is still in my possession, was my constant companion. Lots of short notes are immortalized in it, without which I would not be able today, to write down precise data and information. It now looks pretty desolate because of the ravages of time have completely gnawed on it! But still I take it gladly at hand. Reminder? Sentimentality? In it the past is still present

In the air is smoke and more smoke

The two hospitals understandably want to surrender without a fight, on hearing explosions, machine gun fire and single gunshots. The bridge, the only link to my sister, was blown up – in the air is smoke and more smoke. We could hear people screaming from one side of the shore to the other.

There was a sudden special allocation of sardines – which given the events of the moment I find simply laughable.

The food storage depot for refugees nearby was released and opened for the population and now large human hamsters began to enter. Even close explosions with fierce thunder and roar didn't keep them from grabbing sacks with flour, sugar, rice, peas, and coffee beans and taking them home. Later one could throughout the area smell coffee beans roasted in frying pans.

My mother with our housewife under the road and was safe, but was horrified. The crazed mob ruthlessly dragged the precious sacks over the stone stairs of the supply dump! Many burst and the costly food was trampled!

The enemy tanks still rolled unopposed and one couldn't even think of sleeping that night. There was no longer any opposition from the German side.The next day, the headquarters of the Americans was already pitched in the city. From every smaller and the larger house flutter large and small white flags. There is a curfew! One can hear nearby shootings. Some units of German troops will not surrender. But the use of aircraft ended this resistance very quickly.

One thing is certain, we will not starve to death the next time! Mr. Vollmer, a soldier in the turmoil of the last war could not read, but had helped the two weak women in getting food from the depot.

Despite being banned some people were running around in the threat of punishment and several times there are sharp shots. We have no water, no electricity, we help ourselves with Hindenburg lights which are like tea-lights.

My husband's 29th birthday was today on April 17th. Where he will probably be on that day? The uncertainty is morbid.

As he told me later, his Panzer Division was part of the Raum Wien command and was surrounded in the Vienna area in the western part of Austria. He was unfortunately shot at by the Austrians who were our comrades, from their houses! The following is sarcasm. So these were our friends, the ones who cried together in chorus the language of 1938 things like: "Sieg heil! We want to make our home in the Reich." The Division succeeded in breaking out of the encirclement was able to proceed westward.

I saw that day which was for me very sad picture: eight trucks rolling with German prisoners of war. But there one stops laughing and becomes more aware of and is permeated with the futility of war.

The military government now adopted all sorts of regulations. Some restrictions were put in place. Weapons of any kind had to be registered, otherwise severe penalties were threatened.

I still had my gun in the possession from which I had not been separated during the whole flight. One afternoon I made my way down to the Mulde River. In a high arc I threw it into the waters, I didn't want to risk anything. God knows I never got into a situation where I had to use it.

Meanwhile, the food had to be given to the Americans. We did not follow this rule. Why do we when we have a child's bed where you can store the food? Meanwhile our small baby sleeps in our bed rather than on a mattress!

Our little darling suddenly has a turn for the worse and breathes short breaths. A woman who is known as a healer says to me: "People look in the stroller and always say: 'Oh how sweet, a pretty doll!' Always think to yourself, Be sure not to be proud." I think to myself, "Kiss my ass. This hard evil breathing will stop by itself." So I tried this counsel, and lo and behold, it helped? Is this hoax or what else?

On April 27, we got new passports from the military government. There was also water and electricity again. We hear American news. Berlin is experiencing many bombings and in the house to house fighting the Russian troops have won. Hitler is dead! Propaganda Minister Goebbels has poisoned his entire family and himself. Surrender was unconditional!

We can't believe everything that we're hearing! We are told of the horrible deeds in the concentration camps. How did that happen? We thought they were re-education camps! [Ed. Translator: The idea or image here is that the concentration camps were run like really strict Bible camps.]

My mother always was gone away sewing, so that we can improve a little on our scarce rations. A woman gave me in 1800 grams of meat at the market. So I sewed two blouses for her. Today in the peak of plenty one is hardly able to grasp what that meant back then!

To come back to the above-"hoax" – an different explanation of the malaise was somewhat different. Since I could no longer breast-feed, I had to change the diet of my baby. The doctor gave a prescription: 1 tin of condensed milk. And that was probably the reason for her improvement.

Grimma,
August 4, 1945
Heidrun, first
recording of our
little daughter.

Yesterday we had a lot of excitement in the house. The host came back from captivity, surprisingly emaciated, and on the brink of collapse. For days there had been a big piece of meat in a vinegar marinade in the pantry – that was now just right for a welcome home menu! We were invited and afterward learned from the cook that the meat was from the horse butcher. My mother, who was quite careful when she thought the food seemed bad, even when we were really hungry we had not dared to fry even a little of it. That noble horse-meat was for them was unthinkable!

And again no day like any other!

On July 2, again towels and flags fluttered in each street. But this time they are red! The Russians have superseded the American occupation and the Town Hall is adorned with the Soviet-star! No day like any other!

Through an acquaintance who had despite difficulty found a chance to go back to in my hometown, I find out that my parents' house had been burned down on May 1st for bonfires. Our old hope of ever seeing our expensive belongings sometime is therefore finally lost. The matter of a possible return home was finished.

Especially my mother was greatly disturbed by this information. She had put her whole work and love put into our beautiful home.

My mother now makes contact with two distant cousins who encourage us to change our place of residence to which we unanimously agree. With a rented van and payment of 100 Reichsmarks we drove to Braunsbedra near Merseburg and found there a very good place to stay, after all quarrels and negotiations with the related offices are taken into consideration.

"Where are the youth? Where is the beautiful life, where is anything cheerful for us?"

As a refugee, how poor I am now in any earthly goods. How easy and fortunate was my childhood and youth. How transitory and fleeting is everything!

My father-in-law wants so much to finally see his grandchild. But a trip under present conditions is as good as impossible. So I took it upon myself one day to go alone on the road to Babelsberg. I squeezed myself at 7 p.m. into a completely over filled train to Berlin. In the morning at 4 o'clock I'm stuck in Pape street. Therefore one must bear in mind that no normal passenger cars were in use, but only simple box cars. There were double fares and Russian inspections. I hide all the way back and pull my head-scarf over my face. It happened, that the Russian inspector would say, "You woman, come with me!" After some time the same women came back, tearful or distressed, and took silently their place again. One can well imagine vividly what happened, of that there can be no doubt.

Meanwhile, our country has been divided into four zones of occupation-in. In the north were the English, in the south were the Americans, the French in the west and in the east were the Russians. So there were now boundaries in Germany that are not so easy to cross.

My husband with some of his comrades marched coming from the Vienna command, where the tanks had to be abandoned, fleeing in the direction of the West. They came up to Upper Franconia. In Naila there was a prisoner of war camp into which they went voluntarily. They needed proper discharge papers, without which they could not again to receive food stamps. But where were they to go from here? How quickly could he find his wife and child? He had identified 75 relatives in Apolda in Thuringia a long time ago, so we were able to connect. A release of the prisoners of war was now possible only in the American occupied territory. He smuggled a list out of the camp with the help of a kitchen assistant in which he offered instruction in English or the French language. The camp commander was of the opinion that the Germans should study and my husband now had the brilliant idea, to give the address of the family housekeeper for his father who lived in Neustadt near Coburg as a destination. It was the only address that was known to him in the West.

They welcomed him willingly and with a borrowed bicycle he went on short rounds in the outlying villages do foreign-language teaching. Finally, people had something for which to live!

In the schools there was shortage of teachers since the former teachers first had to be "denazified". He was appointed by the military government as a temporary – public schoolteacher and so came to be a teacher and director of the elementary school after Rothenhof, located near Coburg.

So here we could be reunited and continue our life together.

Over many detours he learned where I was now living with our child. He sent Sister Luise, a former deaconess, on her way, to join us for a very complicated journey.

She brought me a long letter with good advice. I should take nothing unnecessary. How could he know that I had only the bare necessities! There is very little I could yet call my own!

The trip

We expected a journey with many obstacles. I bought a baby buggy for 49.50 Reichsmarks, so Sister Luise could easily transport my belongings. I myself had little Heidrun in her stroller and we took a bus to Naumburg, and stayed there for one night in a hotel room at the station. As agreed, we wanted to ride at 4 o'clock in the morning in a three-wheeled transporter to the border at Kirchgandern for a payment of 300 Reichsmark and to go into the English occupied territory from there. Every day several hundred people passed through the barrier at this point and we wanted to do the same.

But that was easier said than done! When we wanted to leave the back door of the hotel, a Russian soldier appeared and he threatened us with a pistol. You can imagine how quickly we closed the large hotel door. We waited and waited and waited until the heavy footsteps finally went away.

At 6 clock we finally dared to retry the "getaway" and went the short distance to the arranged meeting place. Thank God, our driver had already counted on difficulties and had waited for us. We were driven to Heilgenstadt and then in the direction of the border on foot.

At the turnpike there was a huge crowd! Some of them stood by their horses and carriages, others waited with their luggage by the trolley or were on foot. We spent a whole day waiting. My child was peaceful and sleeps. Then we were loaded on trucks and brought to the Friedland train station. The most difficult part of our trip is now behind us.

But what surprises life gives! Sister Luise suddenly held a sobbing man with a beard in her arms. It was her formerly mis-

December 1945
In Rothenhof – our sunshine Heidrun

sing husband, released from the captivity, that she's run into here. One can hardly believe how life has played itself out.

In Friedland, at the detention center, we had to line up until evening and wait our turn to allow others to register. We are assigned quarters and have to stay in a large hall. Our small golden child's behavior is always exemplary and I prepared her a meal on a small alcohol stove.

On November 2, at 7:30 p.m we are finally sitting on the train. In Eichenberg there is an American check point and to our horror Luise's husband is not allowed to pass because he has no discharge papers. So we unload all the luggage out again and I wait until Sister Luise travels to Gottingen where she will rejoin me. Her husband needs to go to Bebra by way of Kassel and in Fulda, where we finally meet.

It's a journey with obstacles! Now we don't get the train connection to Coburg and all our attempts to somehow get a car failed. We have to remain on Sunday in the Fulda area for the weekend.

On Monday, after a few American check points, we arrive around noon in Coburg. Two women picked me up, because my husband is on the way to teach his private lessons.

In the evening he was surprised by our arrival. He hadn't expected us yet! He couldn't believe that after so long a time he could finally hold us close in his arms!

But after the long uncertainty the anxious life seems to have come to an end. Our life as a couple can begin now and somehow we will do our best to master it.

The school in Rothenhof

The sad life seems to end

In Rothenhof we were given a very friendly welcome by the people living there. The school apartment stood empty and we could get it ready in about eight days.

The Mayor sent around two school children and we were supported with collected household goods. We had literally nothing. We got bedroom furniture borrowed from Neustadt, coupons for a couch, a saucepan and a colander came to us. From Mönchröden came a bunch of yellow organza from a doll factory. I quickly sewed on a borrowed sewing machine a variety of curtains. As things turned out, sometimes they had pleats, sometimes they had frills.

I still had available from my shoulder bag a big part of my money capital from our flight. I got from Mr. Postel three American blankets for 300 Reichsmark. They were a dark color and I had a carpenter make and upholster with them a couch and two armchairs, which now proudly adorned our living room! All the fun cost me 1800 Reichsmarks. We were super-lucky with this achievement!

We were going to come to our first Christmas so far from home. We decorated a beautiful Christmas tree together. However, many things were temporary,but we were completely satisfied with what had been achieved. Our little one was "over the moon" with the beautiful candles and borrowed decorations. Our child was a very quiet and sweet girl and gave us a lot of happiness.

I had always been a big fan of the great Swede Zarah Leander, knew all her songs and watched her movies wherever they

January 1946
This picture was taken already in the New Year.

were shown. The movie "The Great Love" impressed me most and the song:

"The world is not finished
even if it is sometimes gray;
Soon it will be colorful and light blue.
Sometimes there are ups and downs,
even when our brain is full.
From that the world will not cease to exist...
people still need it."

How often I have had this song running through my mind. There ,s so much truth in it.

In February 1946, my father was released from prisoner of war camp. We were the only place he could go in the West, in which he could be settled by the Red Cross. My other family was still in the Russian-occupied territory. He had come from his war effort in Sicily and had been a farm worker in the Rhineland until he found us. Now a further period of waiting was ahead for him.

My husband celebrated his 30th birthday! We had a great and unexpected surprise: The students left an Easter basket on the desk, filled with 40 eggs, a pound of bacon and bouquets! Only those who know the lean times of the past, know how to measure what this gift meant for us. Our menu improved immediately. We can start baking preparing omelets and other egg dishes.

I was already planning what could be sown and planted in a garden. In addition, in the school garden were fruit trees and we already dreaming of plum cake, plum-marmalade and desseerts! There was a little piece of land we could use to grow potatoes. How wonderful everything is now that we have enough to eat!

In June I received a telegram from my sister, whose husband

*Star recording
in 1946*

1947

Heidrun was proud to show her rocking duck. We bought it in exchange for two dress shirts. That was a joy. She was a very quiet and dear girl and gave a lot of joy.

has been released from the Giessen refugee camp. He too survived the war unscathed and intended again to enter the police service. Now everything is completely joy and gladness.

My life went on here in an orderly way in the rural environment, and was really joyful. We still have a lot of friends and acquaintances from that time. Children's parties were organized, we created a theater group. We were pleased to travel with the skillful performances even to some of the surrounding villages! We had a great attendances with "The Spanish Fly" and "Here Meyer – Who's There". In the post-war period there were not many attractions of this sort.

After the currency reform

So the time went by. 1948, we had the monetary reform. There was an entry fee of 40 German marks per person and while the transactions up to that time had shown a large shortage, we could now buy everything in abundance.

On July 23, In 1949, our second daughter Sylvia was born, a sturdy nine pounds, like myself 23 years ago. I was quite disturbed when I got a post-partum fever that came over me that kept everyone on their toes. My mother came and took care of me and my small family.

Our Sylvia grew rapidly, was always cheerful and inclined later to all sorts of pranks. Once she could get a pair of scissors, she snipped and cut about everything. Even the carpet fringe wasn't safe from her! And she found it especially a pleasure to cut the flowers out of my tablecloth!

"Aunt Alma", often passed by the school and when she collected food for her rabbits in a bag, she sometimes "kidnapped"

Our first car, a BMW

August 1949
Our second child has arrived: Sylvia.

from the garden. However, it wasn't long before I had to closely watch her because she had been spoiled with such kinds of goodies by the life style of her family house!

My husband now had to let his job go to the denazified teachers in place. What was going to happen now?

He became self-employed as a sales representative for the wholesale trade: food and delicacies. He represented a whole lot of good suppliers, primarily from the coast, and put in a lot of work on a new life. A set of wheels also had to be found and we purchased our first car – a BMW, from a veterinarian!

My free time was very tight, I always had a lot to do but there was happiness in everything. I always sewed everything for the family, dresses, skirts, sweaters were knitted, not to mention cooking and baking, home-working and in addition was now added the telephone reception service and office work for my husband.

His brother Otto came back from internment from India. He still had connections with a chemist named Weidhase who also could also make connections with companies well know to him.

I had already been known for industriousness at home when I was with my mother. I could not sit still. My Aunt Emma whom we had found in Münchberg after our flight always said, "You're like a squirrel"

When we had to vacate the school accommodation for the new teachers, we moved to a new building, living in Oeslau. Unfortunately, there was still the mold on the walls.

We could not stay there long, because in 1956 we learned that I was pregnant for the third time. We moved to a 4-bedroom apartment near Ahorn, where our Sabine was born. With her our "three-girl-house" was complete! She was born on October 19th, a smooth eight pounds on the scale. Now there was plenty of life in the house!

Picture of the school group
Children's Festival 1948 – Rothenhof School
Our small Heidrun is of course completely excited.

1949 – Heidrun goes to children's carnival.
I quickly made a dress from a bed sheet and decorated it with many colorful silk bows. For lack of other materials it is required to know how to help ourselves! She was totally seriously and proudly looked into the camera.

79

Sylvia 1950

Sylvia 1953

Sylvia 1955
First school day

In 1956, in July,
the offspring is
already included
...

Heidrun and little Sabine
And in Sabine's screams
already in December for
her bottle of milk

What we wrote in the year 1956

Thirty years have passed since I was born: 1926 to 1956. What time! They have been years full of fear, work, escape but also happiness and satisfaction. They have been years of both joyful experiences and sadness. It's been a life lived that it was worth it after all. They hold many memories that are one's only companion in quiet hours.

Thirty years – they should now be followed by a better thirty years without fear and war. How will they be?

There was not one day that was like any other!

Helma Oelwein

Appendix

*Letters from Kurt Oelwein
to his wife Helma Oelwein*

Letter 1
Lower Gaglow, 01/27/1945

My beloved Helma,

I was overjoyed when I received your two dear letters and cards at the same time. I'm more than surprised about the speed of the mailing. Hopefully you have gotten my last letter as quickly.

My dearest, when I hear from you, my mind is relieved, I am glad and happy if I can think of you, and if you are as much in love as I am with you, then I am concerned about my beloved wife. I'm just not indifferent to people and maybe also take things much too seriously, but it's better so than if we take things too carelessly. The time as a soldier has allowed me to think about certain things like a little stubborn will. Some things I see differently now than I would have otherwise; maybe I've learned from my bad luck during my time in the army to think differently about things.

Other people may have an inferiority complex; but thank God I am a long way away from that.

You have to hold belief in yourself and I've never lost that; I am aware as well, that the knowledge and skills of my upbringing which I acquired before the war have served me well in my life and handling things. I would not change places with so many officers. Maybe it was a good thing that I got to know the bad sides of life otherwise one would see everything in a rosy light.

Oh, I long for the end of the war, so one can finally replace the uniforms with civilian clothes. If everything is set right again, then can begin for both of us a blessed and happy time that we want to enjoy to the fullest. But our children should never experience such a hard and difficult childhood-time, as we've once been through it.

The main thing in these decisive days and weeks is the serious commitment to keep our head up and proceed to look straight ahead. Then we will master our fate come what may!!

In the meantime, here at present nothing much has changed. The F.G.B. (Leader Grenadier Brigade) has not yet arrived. They have been on their way for so long already. There's not much news from here. The whole day from morning to evening, from 7 to 5 clock we are trained and reviewing or learning new features of the radio and telephone.

Your concerns, in case of an evacuation about being transported by train, are quite justified. When I left Sagan, I saw for myself the confusion and the misery of the refugees in the stations and on the trains. I was thinking also about you and saw how impossible it would be for you do deal with these crowds. Now, an evacuation of Lower Silesia is hardly in question for the near future. It would likely have come with a new large-scale attack by the Russians. In the big picture, the advance of the enemy as I can see it has been broadly stopped.

Of course it's true that you are going to have to be prepared. If you can get hold of a horse and carriage, that would be very nice. Hopefully Grunert is available for the crucial moment and that he keeps his promise! You won't be able to pack much. Will

Grunert be with you, if it should come to that for leaving? It's much better if a man is with you.

So, as I said, I think the situation at the moment is not very critical.

I have not received any mail from my dad. Meanwhile, have you heard anything from your dad?

Please just be well, don't get sick and do not catch cold!

My health is very good and my cold is completely gone.

I don't know anything more to write about than to tell you than that I love you very much. My thoughts are always with you and our child. Papa will indeed to see it so very soon!

Take many, loving kisses from forever from
Kurt

Heartfelt greetings to Mama and Elfriede.

Letter 2
O.U., 30.1.1945 (O.U. = local accommodation)

My beloved, small, sweet wife!

You can't imagine how happy I was yesterday and the day before yesterday to hear your sweet voice!

I'm so glad that you're doing well. Hopefully everything now will turn out well.

As I already told you, major counter-attack are being planned. I can't say more than that by letter.

The Fuhrer will speak tonight. In any case, keep the necessities ready in case you need it to get away, even if only temporarily. I had no idea that the rail transport is in such a jam.

Given the state of the tracks, the trip for you and the children would be suicidal. One can only feel sorry for the refugees that run through here by horse and cart. Terrible conditions prevail in this regard. I'm not going to give you the details. You may imagine for yourself.

Yes, my darling, you can imagine my concern for you. We should have left earlier for Apolda. But if it were so, no one could have guessed and there can even now be nothing to it. The people in the telegraphic office yesterday and today told me they would make a big effort to help me. Yesterday I had the connection already after five minutes. Today, I went directly to the telegraph office and spoke with the supervisor, told all sorts of things (you know how I can persuade people) in order to obtain the connection. Today, incidentally, all private calls were blocked. So they really made a huge exception with me and then we were able to talk for so long! How beautiful it was! I am relieved somehow. I'm actually become more confident again, but you never know anything for certain and surprises are indeed no longer a rarity. This will work itself out. But it's not really the best. I am also glad that I still was able to spend such a great holiday with you. I'm so indescribably happy that I have you !! Never will anyone be able to disturb our marital bliss! But we are so full of love, right? So, now I'm going to wait for the Fuhrer Hitler's speech and then go to bed. Last night we were awakened already at half past three.

Be embraced with great fondness and many times kissed intimately only by your husband.

Cordial greetings to Mama and Elfriede.

My beloved kitten Helma!

With your two dear letters of the 29th and 30th, which landed quickly here, have you made me very happy! Each line from you is a great pleasure for me and the sun will shine for me every time I hold a letter from you in my hands. That's the way I have loved you but also I would probably be more happy if I knew you were somewhere safe. But in the next few days will probably bring something different.

My unit is still not here. The yesterday's alarm is over. Only other units have moved away. So I still have still the opportunity to get back to my old unit – but I don't know when? Well, you have to wait and see how everything works out. A lot of replacements who belong to the Division, have arrived and live here initially because they cannot reach their units. A good friend of mine, Walter Regler with whom I went from Magdeburg to Cologne early in 1942, has died. I've might have told you about him once. Nothing much new happens here, Only the flow of refugees continues unabated. There is a lot of misery to be seen.

For now I'm not living in the barracks but am back again in my old private quarters. In Steinau the Russians were again beaten back and at the moment there is probably no danger for you. I got the thick turtleneck sweater you sent that keeps me wonderfully warm. Well, my dear, tomorrow I shall write to you again more.

Let me gently embrace you and give you many tender kisses. Kurt.

Cordial greetings to Elfriede and Mama.

My most beloved Helma!

Today I'm going to march to a 10 km distant village with the troop. I do not understand all that. The Russian penetrates farther and we aren't put to use. The advance units of my old unit are supposed to be here. We can expect to daily to be used.

Yesterday there wasn't possible to make phone calls,. All connections were blocked and the same is true today. In addition, no one is allowed to go to Cottbus. I'm so much worried about you. If only everything proceeds smoothly! Last night the snow melted a lot. Rain does that, and the Russians, however, can also no longer do what they want but neither can we.

I only hope that Neuhammer is spared. Also Berlin becomes the front area. At this time I have not gotten a return note from Papa. Otto will also worry about us. He is now is confined in a better kept internment camp in India.

Your Ohlauer relatives are now also scattered to the four winds. How much grief and misery has befallen the German people! As soon as the opportunity presents itself, I'll come to you. But for the time being there is no chance at all.

Only stay healthy and see that nothing happens to you. Right now, I'm safer here than you are in Neuhammer. The Russian are now far north-west of you. Hopefully you will at least get my letters! The letter of the 23rd. It has indeed taken long to very long to get to you. Tomorrow I'll write again. Maybe I can then report something new.

For today let me hug and kiss you tenderly forever loving you By your Kurt.